I Keep Kosher

by **Tami G. Raubvogel** and **Rebecca Schwartz**

book design by **Shepsil Scheinberg**

illustrated by **Tova Katz**

Hachai
PUBLISHING

I KEEP KOSHER

For Aaron and Sara.   T.G.R.

Because every meal means a choice.   R.S.

Dedicated to my son, Shimon, who works as a mashgiach Kashrut.   T.K.

● ● ●

First Edition – 5771 / 2011

Editor: D.L. Rosenfeld
Managing Editor: Yossi Leverton
Layout: Moshe Cohen

ISBN 978-1-929628-52-0
LCCN: 2010912783

Hachai Publishing
Brooklyn, New York
Tel: 718-633-0100
Fax: 718-633-0103
info@hachai.com
www.hachai.com

Printed in China - Xing L01 10/2010

I keep kosher every day
In my toy kitchen, when I play.

Milk and meat can never mix,

Today I'll be the one who picks!

One set of dishes will not do,
Just like Mommy, I have two!

One set for milk, one set for meat,

Now we can both pretend to eat!

Keeping kosher every day
Means eating in a special way.

Not just any meat is fine
In a kitchen that's like mine.

A kosher butcher packs the meat,
Beef and chicken I can eat.

After eating meat, I wait –
No cheese or pizza on my plate.

I count six hours, only then,
Will it be time for milk again!

Keeping kosher every day
Means eating in a special way.

If fins and scales are on a fish,
It goes on a kosher dish.

Salmon, flounder-sole, and trout
Are kosher fish without a doubt!

Fruits and vegetables taste great
On either type of kosher plate.

And no matter where they grow,
Tree or garden, high or low,
They are kosher; now you know.

Keeping kosher every day
Means eating in a special way.

When I shop for kosher treats,
Cookies, candies, snacks and sweets,
I check the package all around,
Until a kosher mark is found!

It's okay to ask a lot,
"May I eat this food or not?"

Keeping kosher every day...

...means eating in a special way!

The ABC's of Kosher… eating in a special way!

A. Kosher means "fit" or suitable for eating, according to Jewish Law. By choosing to eat in accordance with G-d's Will, the Jewish People have the power to elevate the act of eating itself, to be in tune with the spiritual aspect of an everyday, mundane, physical necessity.

B. Kosher meat comes only from animals that chew their cud and have split hooves. Only certain parts of the animal are kosher cuts.

C. For the meat to be kosher, it must be slaughtered, soaked, and salted in a prescribed manner.

D. For milk to be kosher, it must come from a kosher animal such as a cow or goat.

E. Kosher fish are those that have both fins and scales. No other sea creatures are kosher.

F. All vegetables, grains, and fruits are kosher, provided they are washed and checked to determine that they are bug free. Wine and grape juices are in a special category, and need kosher certification.

G. Kosher birds are those listed in the Torah. No birds of prey are on the list.

H. For eggs to be kosher, they must come from kosher birds, and be checked to ensure that they are free of blood spots.

I. Meat foods and dairy foods are always kept separate. Meat is cooked separately from dairy products, in separate pots and pans. They are served on separate sets of dishes, and those utensils are not washed in the same dishwasher. Meat and dairy foods may not be eaten as part of the same meal, even if they are in separate dishes and the correct waiting time has been observed.

J. The separation between meat and dairy includes a waiting time between eating one and the other. The most common waiting time is one half to one hour after milk or soft cheeses (longer for hard, aged cheeses) before consuming meat, and six hours after meat, before consuming milk.

K. Fruits, vegetables, grain, rice, pasta, bread, and other foods that contain neither milk nor meat are called "pareve," and may be eaten either with a dairy meal or with a meat meal.

L. Factories that produce kosher food must have a "mashgiach" (kosher supervisor) who visits repeatedly, and often unannounced, to make sure that all kosher laws are being observed. The organizations that are responsible for such supervision have their specific "hechsher" (supervision) symbol printed right on the package.

M. Kosher restaurants, hotels, and cafeterias with the highest standards will have a "mashgiach t'midi" (supervisor on the premises at all times) to make sure that kosher laws are strictly observed. All kosher eateries have a current kosher certificate, prominently displayed.

There are many more details about keeping kosher than could be included in this note. For more information or to find someone to help make your kitchen kosher, contact your local Orthodox rabbi.